Peter Pan

PaRragon

Bath · New York · Singapore · Hong Kong · Cologne · Delhi · Melbourne

Deep in the heart of London was the house where the Darling family lived.

Wendy Darling shared a nursery with her two younger brothers, John and Michael.

At bedtime, Wendy told her brother stories about a faraway place – Never Land.

The hero of these stories was Peter Pan, a boy who never grew up! Peter's special friend was a tiny fairy called Tinkerbell.

John and Michael loved to act out these stories in which Peter had wonderful adventures.

One night, when the children were fast asleep, Peter Pan and Tinkerbell flew in through the nursery window. They had come to search for Peter's shadow. It had escaped the night before while Peter was listening at the window to one of Wendy's stories.

Just then, Wendy woke up. She was thrilled to meet Peter Pan and agreed to help him and Tinkerbell capture the mischievous shadow.

Wendy told Peter that tonight was her last night in the nursery. Because she was growing up, Wendy was to have a bedroom of her very own.

"Fly with me to Never Land," Peter urged. "You never have to grow up there!" Wendy agreed at once, as long as her brothers could come too!

So, Peter told Wendy, John and Michael to each think a wonderful thought. Then he shook Tinkerbell over them, sprinkling them with magic pixie dust.

Before they knew it, the excited children were soaring high above the rooftops of London.

"We'll take the second star to the right and fly straight on until morning," Peter called, leading the way.

But, by the time the children flew over the enchanted world of Never land, all was not well. Tinkerbell was becoming jealous of Wendy - Peter seemed to like her far too much!

Without waiting for the others, Tinkerbell flew straight to Peter's hideout. This was where his friends, the Lost Boys, also lived.

The spiteful fairy told the Lost Boys that a terrible Wendy Bird was heading their way - and that Peter had ordered them to attack it.

When Peter and the Darling children flew into sight, the Lost Boys used their catapults and peashooters to knock the Wendy Bird out of the sky.

Luckily, Peter managed to catch Wendy before she crashed to the ground! He was furious with Tinkerbell. As a punishment, he sent the naughty fairy away for a week.

Later that day, Peter sent John, Michael and the Lost Boys off to capture Indians while he took Wendy on a tour of the island.

The boys set off on their adventure and soon arrived in a clearing in the middle of a wood. "We must surround the enemy and take them by surprise," John whispered.

But the Indians had disguised themselves as trees and took the boys by surprise instead! The boys were captured and taken back to the Indian village.

Meanwhile, Peter had taken Wendy to the beautiful Mermaid Lagoon. Suddenly, Peter spotted a little rowing boat in the distance. "Why, it's Captain Hook!" he cried.

Captain Hook was a wicked pirate and Peter Pan's greatest enemy.

Once, in a fierce battle, Peter had cut off Hook's hand. The pirate now had a terrible steel hook screwed to his left wrist.

A hungry crocodile had eaten the pirate's hand. He had enjoyed his meal so much that he now followed Hook everywhere, hoping for a chance to gobble up the rest of him!

Peter and Wendy followed Hook as he headed towards Skull Rock. Peter was shocked to see the Indian Princess, Tiger Lily, in the boat too. He and Wendy watched as Hook tied the Princess to a rock in the sea. Peter knew he had to help.

"If you don't tell me where Peter Pan's hideout is," the wicked pirate snarled at Tiger Lily, "I'll leave you here to drown!"

Tiger Lily was very frightened but she refused to betray her friend.

12

Suddenly, Peter flew in front of Hook. "You again!" the Captain cried, rushing at Peter with his sword.

Up and down the rocky cliffs they fought. Then, Hook slipped and only just managed to grab hold of the rocks to stop himself from falling into the sea. Down below, the crocodile snapped hungrily.

Mr Smee, the boatman, rushed over and pulled Hook into his rowing boat. As Mr Smee hastily rowed back to the pirate ship, the crocodile was snapping right behind them!

Peter and Wendy rescued Tiger Lily and took her home.

The Indian Chief had been very worried about his daughter and was overjoyed to see her safe. To thank Peter, he set John, Michael and the Lost Boys free and named Peter an Honorary Chief.

At last, tired out after their adventures, Peter and the children returned to Peter's secret hideout.

Meanwhile, Captain Hook was back on his ship trying to get warm. He was furious that Peter Pan had outwitted him again.

All of a sudden, Hook thought of a brilliant plan! He had discovered that Peter was cross with Tinkerbell and had sent her away for a week. So, the wicked pirate ordered Mr Smee to bring the little fairy to the ship that very night.

That evening, Hook welcomed Tinkerbell on-board his ship. He told her that he needed her help to catch Wendy. All she had to do was show Hook where Peter's hideout was.

Tinkerbell was delighted to help. She dipped her toes in a bottle of ink and danced across a map of Never Land. Her footprints clearly showed the way to Peter's hideout.

Hook smiled. He grabbed Tinkerbell and locked her in a glass lantern. At last, he could get his revenge on Peter Pan once and for all!

Back at Peter's hideout, Wendy, John and Michael were feeling homesick.

"I want my mother," sobbed Michael. And although the Lost Boys didn't know what a mother was, they decided they wanted one too. So, Wendy promised that they would all go back to her London home together.

Peter didn't want to leave Never Land and grow up. He watched gloomily as his friends waved goodbye.

"Goodbye, Peter," said Wendy before she left. "I'll never forget you."

But Captain Hook and the other pirates were outside the hideout. The pirates captured the children and took them back to Hook's ship where they tied them to the ship's mast.

Before Hook returned to the ship, he left a parcel for Peter. It had a label on it that said,

To Peter,
With love from Wendy.

Back on-board his ship, Hook snarled at the children. "You have a choice, either sign your name in my book and join my pirate band or walk the plank!" he said.

The boys quite liked the idea of becoming pirates, but Wendy didn't. "Peter Pan will save us!" she said.

Hook laughed loudly. "Peter Pan won't save you this time," he sneered. "We left a surprise present for him – a bomb! Very soon he'll be blown out of Never Land for ever!"

Hearing these words, Tinkerbell knew she had to warn Peter. She struggled in her glass prison. Suddenly, there was a loud – **CRACK!** The glass lantern broke and Tinkerbell was free!

The tiny fairy reached Peter's hideout just as he was about to open the parcel. She grabbed the bomb and threw it as far away as she could. Seconds later, there was a huge explosion.

Then, Tinkerbell told Peter that Wendy and the others were in danger. Peter sped off to rescue them with Tinkerbell close behind.

Meanwhile, Hook had forced Wendy to walk the plank. When she stepped off the plank everybody waited for the SPLASH as she hit the water. But it never came. Peter Pan had arrived just in time to lift Wendy safely back onto the ship! He turned to face his enemy.

There was a loud crash of steel as Peter's dagger and Hook's sword met. Back and forth they went in the most terrible battle ever fought.

Still fighting, they climbed up to the top of the ship's rigging. Hook lunged at Peter, who fought back, finally forcing the Captain to slip and fall backwards.

Waiting for him in the water below was the hungry crocodile. The children clapped and cheered as they watched Hook trying to escape the crocodile's snapping jaws.

Hook spotted Mr Smee in the rowing boat, and swam towards him. But the crocodile was right behind - and catching up!

As Hook disappeared into the distance, Peter gave the order to raise the anchor. Then, Tinkerbell sprinkled the pirate ship with magic pixie dust.

In no time at all, the ship was soaring high above Never Land and heading back towards London.

Soon, Wendy, John and Michael were
safely back in the nursery.

    And up in the sky, silhouetted against the
full moon, was the outline of the pirate ship.
    Peter Pan, Tinkerbell and the Lost Boys
(who weren't quite ready to grow up yet), were off
on another wonderful adventure.